P9-BIL-740

Madokoro, Hisako, 1938-
Buster's first thunderstorm

DO NOT REMOVE
CARDS FROM POCKET

OCT 1 0 1991

ALLEN COUNTY PUBLIC LIBRARY

FORT WAYNE, INDIANA 46802

You may return this book to any agency, branch,
or bookmobile of the Allen County Public Library.

DEMCO

BUSTER'S
first thunderstorm

By Hisako Madokoro   English text by Patricia Lantier   Illustrated by Ken Kuroi

**For a free color catalog describing Gareth Stevens' list of high-quality children's books,
call 1-800-341-3569 (USA) or 1-800-461-9120 (Canada).**

Library of Congress Cataloging-in-Publication Data

Madokoro, Hisako, 1938-
   [Korowan to gorogoro. English]
   Buster's first thunderstorm / text by Hisako
Madokoro ; illustrations by Ken Kuroi.
      p.   cm. — (The Adventures of Buster the puppy)
   Translation of: Korowan to gorogoro.
   Summary: Buster the puppy ignores the warning
signs as all the animals around him prepare for an
approaching thunderstorm.
   ISBN 0-8368-0493-7
   [1. Dogs—Fiction.   2. Thunderstorms—Fiction.
3. Animals—Fiction.]   I. Kuroi, Ken, 1947-   ill.
II. Title.   III. Series: Madokoro, Hisako, 1938-
Korowan. English.
PZ7.M2657Bw   1991
[E]—dc20   90-47869

North American edition first published in 1991 by
Gareth Stevens Children's Books
1555 North RiverCenter Drive, Suite 201
Milwaukee, Wisconsin 53212, USA

This U.S. edition copyright © 1991.   Text
copyright © 1991 by Gareth Stevens, Inc.   First
published as *Korowan To Gorogoro* (*Korowan and
the Lightning*) in Japan with an original copyright
© 1989 by Hisako Madokoro (text) and Ken Kuroi
(illustrations).   English translation rights arranged
with CHILD HONSHA through Japan Foreign-
Rights Centre.

All rights reserved.   No part of this book may
be reproduced or used in any form or by any
means without written permission from Gareth
Stevens, Inc.

Cover design: Kristi Ludwig

Printed in the United States of America

2 3 4 5 6 7 8 9 97 96 95 94 93 92 91

Gareth Stevens Children's Books
MILWAUKEE

Allen County Public Library
Ft. Wayne, Indiana

2

One day, Buster and his
friend Snapper were
playing when the sky
began to grow dark.

"I'm scared," said Snapper.
"I want to go home."

"I wonder what Snapper is
afraid of," Buster thought.
"Maybe these little chicks will
play with me."

The baby chicks played
hide-and-seek on Buster's
head. "Wheee! This is fun!"

No one worried about the
dark clouds.

"A storm is coming!"
Mother Hen cried.
"Everybody home!"

The chicks peeped
good-bye to Buster, and
then he was alone again.

Black clouds rumbled
across the sky.

Buster suddenly noticed
little black creatures
running up and down
the flowers.

10

12

Buster asked the army of ants to play. "We want to get home before the rain comes," the ants cried. "You'd better hurry home, too!"

Suddenly the whole sky
turned black. Buster saw two
yellow butterflies trying to fly
in the strong wind.

Flash! Crash! Lightning
and thunder filled the
summer sky.

Buster shut his eyes
and curled himself into
a fuzzy ball.

"I'm scared!" he yelped.
"I want to go home, too!"

Buster winked and blinked to keep the rain out of his eyes.

"Grab onto my coat!" he called out to the butterflies. "Let's go to my house!"

The rain fell harder and
harder as Buster
raced home.

"There you are!" said his
mother happily.

Buster was glad to be home. He felt warm and cozy snuggled up against his mother.

The rain soon stopped,
and the sky was sunny
and blue again. Buster was
ready for a new adventure.

24